PRISONERS
OF THE
MIND

J. Kent Johnson

PAGE PUBLISHING
Conneaut Lake, PA

First originally published by Page Publishing 2023

ISBN 979-8-88960-394-8 (pbk)
ISBN 979-8-88960-396-2 (digital)

Printed in the United States of America

To our volunteer servicemen who often experience war and return home wounded by post-traumatic stress.

To Dr. Tammy Ricker, licensed marriage and family therapist, who helped me escape my rabbit hole during a lifetime crisis.

To my family—Terri, Genevieve, James, and Michael, whose love and understanding aided my recovery from depression and a childhood trauma.

PREY

Men are not prisoners of fate, but only
prisoners of their own minds.
—Franklin D. Roosevelt

Only the lifting of the predawn crimson mask reveals clues to the secrets of the continuing struggle.

A cat screams its last challenge to love's rival; a dog howls soulfully at the vanishing sky crescent. Rats scurry toward nest shelters inside twisted hulks of wrecking-yard cars and trucks, many of which burn in their rust until the approach of yellowing dawn.

Some of the rodents are bloated from their nightly visits to the produce market next door to the wrecking yard. Others are scraggly and gaunt and hobble in retreat, bleeding and scarred from battles lost over mildewed lettuce, decaying celery, or soggy beets.

One of the produce-market war veterans is anxious about his long and hazardous return to a home that has become contested and more insecure in this struggle. A scream from overhead goes unheeded by the rat in his maddening worry. A huge onion-eyed owl swoops down for its final nocturnal killing.

Nearby, another predator, a silhouette in the rising sun, sinks its jaws into its prey, first puncturing, then ripping the victim's tough shell-like skin. The bucket of the wrecking-yard crane gnaws deeply.

The bite is crushing. The act is sudden, too swift even for death throes.

The beast straightens to its full height amid the carnage and turns to sling the carcass away as if in distaste. It rears, pauses momentarily as if to confirm that it is still master, then turns back again to claim another victim, to renew what's to become a day-long ritual of retribution.

Jerry, an old man in his late sixties, jerks back on the clutch lever with both hands to bring the massive movable machine to a halt. A pull by his right hand frees the winch cable, and the cable reel squeals as the huge-jawed bucket drops onto another wreck.

The crash is thunderous. The bucket's teeth screech as they tear through the car's steel skin. The auto's headliner and its padding protrude from the

The old man seems at one with the beast.

wound. Oil seeps bloodily from somewhere within the mutilation onto the wrecking-yard ground.

The old man seems at one with this beast and is brutal, almost enthusiastic, in his task of smashing the car bodies and stacking them onto adjacent railroad cars. The crane whips around to get another car, and one of its steel tracks lifts off the ground; the crane appears on the verge of tipping over as the weight of the boom, the bucket plus the car body, threatens its stability.

Outside the wrecking yard, Sam stares at the fantastic scene through a hole in the wrecking-yard fence. Unable to enter because of a locked gate, he waves without success to get the old man's attention.

Sam starts to turn away, for it's time for him to start work at the produce market, but something about the drama intrigues him, and he pauses to study the operator and machine. It may be a window into the past; for an instant, Sam thinks, the scene seems prehistoric.

The crane is old like its operator. And like the old wrecks it is moving, it, too, is unprotected and at the mercy of the ravages of time. It has not been painted in many years, and rust bloodies the crane cab and boom where the old paint has peeled away.

Jerry is lean and hard. His skin gleams from the sweat of working inside the crane's hot cabin. A red fungus of a beard hides his facial features, and only a jagged scar escapes the blight of hair. The scar is narrow at its source, above the right cheekbone inside the hairline, and enlarges like a sea-bound river until it is obscured by the unkempt long beard. This hair frames the remainder of Jerry's face, emphasizing a gaunt look and exaggerating an already deeply set pair of eyes and the tightness of his skin. The exposed face seems fleshless. The eyes appear empty.

On the top of this skull is a deteriorating hard hat Sam had seen the old man wearing the day before. Sam wondered why the old man still wore it. It obviously would no longer provide any protection. It has a large dent on the side above the right ear, and a jagged rip runs through the middle of the dent. The hat, too, is stained red.

"If he was wearing that hat when it was damaged like that," Sam says softly to himself, "how did he survive?"

Sam's wonderings suddenly are broken by the crash of the bucket claws and the collapse of the top of another car. Sam waves again. But Jerry doesn't notice; so absorbed is he in his task.

"Well, I'll have to try again after I get off work," Sam says to himself as he turns and walks toward the produce market. "I don't want to forget what happened last night."

He briskly moves from the employee parking area across fifty yards of asphalt to the market's loading dock where he will spend most of his day. Two truck trailers, left from the day before, await their unloading. Their refrigeration compressors hum above everything else for the day is still awakening.

SHARECROPPER'S SON

As Sam reaches the loading dock, he hears a *pop, pop, pop* from the exhaust of a diesel truck as it slows down to enter the produce-market gates, then hears the driver grind a gear in shifting down. Sam's day starts. It's 6:30 a.m.

"They're starting early today," Sam remarks. "Looks like it'll be another busy one."

As Sam starts his work, the old man mechanically continues his tedious task. The vigor of his work and the fearful crushing of the carcasses awaken deep-seated feelings for Sam.

Sam is sixty-two and, like many of his generation, has experienced the hard times of the post-Depression years: hunger as a sharecropper's son, the death of his father when he was thirteen, working in the broiling cotton fields of Texas as a child.

Sam had to quit school at fourteen and go to work to help support his mother and younger brothers and sisters when his older brothers started families of their own. Then came the Depression-era Civilian Conservation Corps (CCC) and afterward World War II.

Photographs of his younger years portray Sam as a happy, muscular young man. Because of his sun-bleached blond hair and his welcoming and pleasing nature, friends called him "Cotton." He developed a strong work ethic while toiling from sunrise to sunset harvesting grain in the Sacramento Valley. But he wanted more.

The CCC represented hope for the future. Training in carpentry, learning to operate machine tools, and electrical engineering offered escapes from back-breaking work on the farm.

But World War II interrupted his training. He joined the Army Air Corps and became a cryptographer. Assigned to Gen. Dwight D. Eisenhower's headquarters in England, he was trained at Oxford University to decode messages and attempt to break Germany's secret codes.

He was assigned to a secret unit and was among thousands of Allied troops who landed in the D-Day invasion of Normandy. He learned to kill.

"I just shined the general's shoes."

When he returned to his wife and son at the end of the war, he was found to be changed, wounded by his experiences like other war veterans who went through such horrors. Only there were no visible scars. He was angry and violent and would strike out unexpectedly at other people like a wounded animal.

Being locked up in a secret communications bunker that was wired with explosives or battling behind the lines must have changed him, his family speculated. But when they asked him to talk about it, to open up, he always clammed up.

"I just shined the general's shoes," he would tell them. "Didn't you know that? I wasn't no hero!"

But Sam's thinking had become warped by war trauma; he was consumed by thoughts of being unworthy. He received uncontrolled abuse from his father when growing up, including beatings and harsh criticism. In the long run, he could be devastated by criticism; and when he accomplished something praiseworthy, he could not savor it. It was as if success in his life was "just an accident."

Because of how he suffered in World War II, he was suspicious of everyone. He was quick to anger, sometimes without an obvious cause, as if he was driven by inner demons. His violence drove his family from him, and because of the isolation that followed, his actions became more extreme. For most of his adult life, he was a loner who couldn't learn from his actions or adjust to society.

Sam also was burdened with pain due to a horrific incident in France after the Normandy invasion.

He and nine of his buddies, many of them also code breakers, rode in a truck one night to the mess hall located on the opposite side of the airstrip near Paris. The group finished their meals and were about to board the truck when a cry of fear was heard.

"It's on fire," one of the men screamed. "It's going to crash!"

All the men looked up and watched a B-17 coming in for a landing. It was burning furiously.

"Get ready. They are going to need help," one of the men exclaimed as he started to run toward the crashing bomber.

"The plane might be still loaded with bombs!" Sam warned.

"We've got to help," another cried out.

The group followed the first man toward the plane which, by now, had crashed and spun around.

Flames quickly engulfed the aircraft as the ten buddies ran to help the crew.

Men were jumping out of hatches to get away. Sam and his buddies were just about twenty yards away when suddenly there was a tremendous

Pain of the crash deaths ruled Sam's life.

explosion. The plane blew apart and was engulfed by flames. It had been carrying nearly a full load of fuel and bombs.

The bomber crew members were on fire as they left the plane. When Sam and his friends approached, almost all of them were caught in the explosion.

The crew of the B-17 was killed as were eight of Sam's buddies. Sam received second-degree burns over much of his body. He was horrified at what he had witnessed and suffered survivor's guilt.

Thereafter, this pain ruled Sam's life. It was an unspeakable experience that he refused to share with his family or friends. He was quick-tempered and would lash out. His anger would cause him to lose six jobs in his life and cost him three marriages.

Through therapy, however, Sam came to realize that his wartime pain was the root of his anger and that he was ill. The disability was not his fault. Just realizing those facts helped him to understand his suffering. The process transformed Sam into a different person. He no longer felt unworthy. The therapy was key to his recovery.

Afterward, he was still somewhat of a loner but had no run-ins with other people. He found success at the food market where he became an assistant manager.

WELCOME "VIRGINIA"

Meanwhile, life also hasn't been easy for Jerry, the old man, and he gives evidence of the venom he's been feeling by manipulating the carcasses onto railroad cars. He had been told by his bosses not to crush the bodies because they still need to be stripped before they are sent to the smelter. His job is just to unload trucks hauling the cars in and put the vehicles onto the flatcars.

"Fuck them," Jerry says of his bosses as he rams another car into a stack of wrecks, knocking them all over. He'll have to restack them.

"Why don't you get your act together"

"It's job security!" Jerry screams with a haunting laugh. "Job security! Fuck them!"

Jerry imagines hearing his wife there in the cab with him, looking over his shoulder.

"You lamebrain. Why don't you get your act together."

"You'll never amount to anything working in that wrecking yard."

"Shut your mouth, Sally," Jerry screams. "You'll get it when I get through tonight, I promise you."

He works mindlessly, but a memory of his wartime experience encroaches. He thinks of his parachute jump behind enemy lines, the pain in his right ankle, which was broken when he hit the ground.

He could only hobble for a hedge row fence with his chute to get away from a German patrol.

But before he could reach safety, an unseen German soldier calls out, "*Achtung!*"

Jerry is just a few feet away as he rounds the end of the hedge barrier.

He sees the German and quickly pulls out his knife. He drives it deeply into the German's midsection and up and behind the sternum. The soldier straightens to his full height, grabs at the knife, and then slumps to his knees before falling onto his side.

Jerry gasps, doubles over. He gets sick

Jerry stares at the wound. Intestines protrude from a gaping hole left behind in the stabbing. Jerry gasps and doubles over. He gets sick.

"Damn them for making us do that," Jerry cries out from the cab just as he's smashing another wreck into another pile, punishing the wreckage in his pain.

Bad memories rule Jerry's mind as he finishes his shift at the wrecking yard and returns home to his wife, Sally. He tosses his crushed hard hat on the sofa, kicks off his boots, and grabs a beer from their fridge.

"Where in the hell have you been, Jerry?" Sally demands. "I fixed dinner, and now it's cold. You are two hours late!"

"Don't give me any of your shit, Sally. I get home when I get home. You don't have anything to say about it," Jerry responds defiantly.

"Why don't you ever think about me, waiting at home," Sally replies. "I'm scared all the time that you'll have had a bad day again and you'll take it out on me!"

"Don't come at me now. I did have a bad day. A guy from the market killed King," Jerry fires back in anger. "King was my best friend."

"Well, I'm glad he's dead." Sally blurts. "All he did was chew up our furniture and mess all around the house, and I had to clean up after him."

"Don't say anything bad about him," Jerry commands as he jumps up from the sofa in defiance and throws the beer he is holding across the room. "It hurts now that he's gone."

"I didn't think anything ever hurt you. You have no heart. In fact, I doubt you can love anything," Sally continues. "You show it every night in bed. It's always a slam, bang, thank you, ma'am. Besides, you have no penis. You can't even see it under your big gut."

"Watch what you say," Jerry screams angrily, taking a few steps toward his wife before stopping and going over to punch the wall. "Someday, on a day like this, I'll fix you. It'll be the last day you'll ever see."

Jerry, still struggling to control himself, walks out of the room.

"Go ahead and leave, you son of a bitch. You aren't even a man," Sally screeches at him.

Anger continues to dominate Jerry's life because of the war trauma he suffered and the accidental death of his cousin when he was a child. According to *The Body Keeps the Score*, research has found that trauma, especially at a young age, changes the brain. And the pain of those experiences is the root of the anger.

But Jerry rejected his doctor's recommendation for him: take his meds, get in a support group for post-traumatic stress disorder (PTSD) victims, and get into therapy. As a result, Jerry remained ruled by his PTSD.

UPWARD CLIMB

The next day, at the produce market across the way, Sam is midway through his morning. He is the new assistant manager for Gardenland where he has worked for twenty years. He joined Gardenland when he was in his forties. He could have finished his war-interrupted college but chose the security of a steady paycheck over the struggle of the unemployment lines. He had a wife and a child whom he had to support, and time wouldn't allow him to go college under the GI Bill.

Now, seven jobs later, he is at Gardenland in charge of the loading docks.

He started as a swamper, loading and unloading trucks by hand, then progressed to forklift operator, truck driver, and loading dock foreman. Next, he moved into the business office as a clerk. But being stuck at a desk wasn't for him, he decided. He took business classes in hopes of becoming a manager.

> **"I always kept my head down."**

The climb had been slow, but Gardenland recognized Sam's diligence and work ethic and rewarded him with an assistant manager's post in its Fresno market. Sam held that job for four years until the market's assistant manager retired.

"I always kept my head down, got to work on time, mastered each job I was assigned," he often taught his children when they asked about his work. "More important was learning what each boss expected of me, and then doing it to the letter."

"Of course, it helped to kiss their asses," he'd punctuate his story, always drawing laughs from whoever was listening.

BANG BANG

Jerry lay facedown in the sand and hugged his rifle; bullets whistled over his head.

"Pinned down," he groaned. "I hate this. Damn!"

"Jones, Rubin, Thorpe," screamed the Sarge above the *rat-a-tat* of a deadly machine gun, concealed in a bunker about one hundred yards away. "Try to flank them on the right. Stirling, Ebbe, Fitch, and Jerry, take the left. The rest of you, give them cover," Sarge ordered.

Jerry felt the bullets whizzing past but knew what he had to do.

Fragments ripped through the foliage. In an instant, he rolled to his left, leaped up, and sprinted to the left of the machine gun, firing his rifle to keep the Germans' heads down.

Jerry heard *twang, twang* as two bullets ricocheted off a nearby rock. He dove behind a clump of bushes, rolled over to his right, and scrambled back to his feet in just seconds. He was just thirty yards away from the bunker when he heard *whomp, whomp*!

Two German grenades had exploded ahead of him and to the right. Jerry dropped to the ground.

Whomp!

Another explosion sent metal fragments ripping through the foliage near Jerry's head.

The machine gun had stopped firing, Jerry realized, and he stopped and listened.

The rest of the squad was still caught in the middle of a clearing in front of the bunker.

"The Krauts were playing dead. And they got Fitch and Stirling," Ebbe cried out from somewhere on the right. "And I'm hit! Medic! Medic!"

"Sons of bitches. I'll get them!" hollered Jerry as he leaped from behind a tree and began a mad dash into the teeth of the firing machine gun.

He grabbed a grenade from his belt as he ran, clinched the pin in his teeth, and jerked with his arm. He hit the dirt, rolled twice, and jumped back up just to the left of the bunker opening. He tossed the grenade inside.

Kaboom!

'I got the motherfuckers. That's for Fitch and Stirling, you ass-holes," Jerry said to himself as he leaped back to his feet and ran around to the bunker entry. He wanted to finish the job. He jumped through the smoke and dust, which

He emptied his M1 into the corpses.

were still belching out of the opening, and leaped inside, firing as he went. He emptied his M-1 into the corpses he found inside.

"We got them, Sarge. All clear!" Jerry yelled.

Then one of the bodies turned over and grinned at Jerry.

"All right, you got us," it said. "Now we get to be the Marines, and you guys are the Krauts."

"Okay, Tommy, but I want to have a tank this time. And you can't use flame throwers," Jerry replied, trying to negotiate the terms of the next battle.

"Hey, that's too hard. Then I get to use a bazooka," Tommy said.

At about that time, Johnny ran up from the clearing where he had been playing Sarge.

"That was great, Jerry. You looked just like that guy in *Sands of Iwo Jima*. You jumped up, bounced left, then rat-a-tat, then kaboom, balooey. You killed them dead," Johnny recalled in glee.

"Yeah, you remember when John Wayne romped toward the machine gun nest in the movie and tossed in that pineapple?" Jerry enthusiastically replied. "Baroom! And it blew one guy right out of the opening. Wow!"

"Right," chimed in Pete, one of the dead Krauts in the bunker. "Remember when they hit the tank with a bazooka, and the guy opens the top and gets out, and he's on fire and everything?"

"No. Don't you remember? That was *Away All Boats*," Johnny corrected.

"Wait. Someone's calling," Jerry called out, interrupting the four boys' musing about war movies they'd seen at the local movie house.

"Jerry…Jerry!"

"Damn it, son of a bitch!" Jerry grumbled. "That's my mom. I've got to go, guys. It's time for lunch."

"Shit! It's only eleven thirty. Can't you wait? We just got started," moaned Tommy.

"No. I've got to go. See you guys later," Jerry answered while starting on a trot for home.

"Yeah. Guess I'd better go too," Johnny added.

"Let's play this again after lunch. Then we can spend some time in our foxhole. We're almost deep enough for a tunnel into another room."

Jerry stopped for a second and turned around to tell them, "I won't be able to do it this afternoon. Maybe tomorrow. My cousins are coming over."

"Next time we get to be the good guys."

"Okay," lamented the boys he left behind.

"Remember, next time we get to be the good guys," Pete shouted after him.

Jerry reached his gate and looked back at his friends. Johnny was on his way home, and Pete was talking to Tommy, who was standing on a giant tractor tire they had pretended was a bunker. Jerry smiled, opened the gate, and went inside.

He ran up to his back porch, stuck the tree limb he used as a rifle into the mud near the faucet, then hung his army helmet on it.

LIKE IN THE MOVIES

"**M**om, I'm home," Jerry yelled as he started inside.

His mom was right there, holding out the peanut butter and jelly sandwich she had prepared.

"That was fun," Jerry murmured as he bit into the sandwich. "Just like the movies."

"You kids are always using those war movies," his mom said. "They'll all lead to trouble someday," she warned.

Jerry had spent most of his summer playing with the same friends. They were all eight years old now; and war, cowboys and Indians, and cops and robbers were their favorite games. All had army helmets they bought down at the army surplus store for $2 each. Everyone had cap pistols but liked to make their own weapons out of sticks and lumber for war.

Saturday afternoon matinees with Tom Mix and Roy Rogers and war movies with John Wayne and Robert Ryan fueled their imaginations with things to do. They played mostly in a corner vacant lot where they had started a foxhole under a lone tree. Up in the tree was a tree house they had built with scrap lumber. That's where they held their meetings and sometimes hid in wait as snipers during war.

The boys were swept up in their imaginings and would spend hours at them. Only a call to come home from someone's mother could stop it unless, of course, they had one of their rare arguments over who shot who first or who was dead.

After lunch, Jerry was sent to clean his room, but he didn't get past the comic books on his bed. He was deep into a GI Joe adventure when he heard his aunt and uncle's car drive up.

He threw the comic book aside, jumped up from the bed, grabbed his Red Ryder BB gun, and proceeded to sneak into the living room where he hid behind the couch.

Ernie and Philip, Jerry's cousins, ran through the front door ahead of the adults.

Jerry lifted and fired. "Blam, blam! Bang, bang! You're dead," he yelled.

Ernie was surprised by the sneak attack but played along.

He first grabbed his shoulder, then his chest, and recoiled from the volley of bullets fired at him. He staggered to his left, twisted around, and fell against the armchair in the corner, bounced off it, and staggered across the room back to the door where he fell flat on his back, dead.

"Blam, blam. Bang, bang. You're dead."

The aunt and uncle entered and nearly tripped on the boy on the floor.

"You kids. Don't play those games in the house. You'll break something," Aunt Opal warned. "Get up, Ernie."

"That was great, Ernie," Jerry said in admiration. "I didn't think you were ever going to die."

After dinner, Jerry's mom told the three boys that the adults were going out for dinner and that they'd be left alone. "I left you spaghetti for supper."

"Jerry and Ernie. You're the oldest, and I expect you both to watch Philip. And I expect you all to behave," she said, waving her finger at each of them to emphasize her point. "Can I trust you kids?"

"Yes, Mom," Jerry replied. Ernie and Philip nodded yes in unison.

The trio had to stay inside where they played board games and took turns at checkers and Canasta.

But they soon tired of that.

"What can we do now," Ernie asked Jerry.

"Just wait here," Jerry answered as he got up and left the room. Several minutes later, he returned carrying a hunting rifle and a German Luger.

"Wow! Your dad's guns. I thought they were locked up," Ernie said.

"They were, but I know where my dad keeps the key."

Jerry put the two guns down on the couch, pointing to one of them. "This one's a pistol that was actually used in World War I," he said of the Luger.

He gestured toward the second gun, a lever-action carbine. "That one is just like my BB gun."

"Are they loaded?" asked Philip.

"No," Jerry replied.

"Let's play war," blurted out Ernie, eager to get his hands on one of the guns.

"Good idea," said Jerry. "But let's listen for my dad's car. They shouldn't be home for a few hours, but they might come home early. I'd really get a licking if they caught us with the guns."

Philip sat out of the game and colored in a coloring book. There weren't enough guns for him.

Jerry and Ernie spent the next hour and a half in a living dream, playing war with real guns. They invented new scenarios as they went along, and they both got killed at least once. They each used their imaginations to their fullest in trying to be the most dramatic: the best at dying.

And Ernie was the best at it. He'd stagger, bounce off walls, trip over footstools, and do flips and rolls. When he died, the other two would just watch and explode into laughter when the make believe was over.

Jerry was starting to get bored, and while holding the carbine, told them he wanted to show them something.

"My dad showed us his guns and let us shoot them," Ernie recalled. "But he doesn't have a carbine."

Jerry pulled a bullet out of his pocket. He had found it in his dad's sock drawer.

"This is how you load it," Jerry continued, shoving the shell into the slot on the side of the carbine.

"My dad showed me," Jerry related before pushing down hard on the gun's lever and pulling it back up. The downward action pushed the bullet up into the chamber where it was ready to fire.

"It's cocked," Ernie said. "Be careful!"

"I will," Jerry assured him. "I'll uncock it. I've seen Dad do this a hundred times."

He hadn't really seen it a hundred times, maybe once or twice, but Jerry was sure he could do what Dad did.

"Be careful. Don't kill me," cautioned Ernie, who had moved up against a wall.

"I won't."

To release the hammer without firing the rifle, Jerry recalled, he had to hold the hammer with his thumb while pulling on the trigger at the same time and then let the hammer down gently.

Everything was happening in slow motion.

But Jerry struggled in his attempt and discovered he couldn't do it with just one hand, so he tried both hands, holding the butt of the gun in the crotch of his arm.

He placed a finger of his left hand on the trigger and the thumb of his right hand on the hammer. But his hands weren't big enough. He was clumsy and his thumb slipped as he pulled the trigger.

Bam!

The report of the rifle deafened Jerry for an instant and left him dazed. The smell of gunpowder permeated the air, and Jerry could hear a loud ringing. There was a smell of gunpowder and copper in the air.

He looked up at his cousins.

Philip, also dazed, stood to the right. His mouth was wide open. A scream was coming out of it, but Jerry couldn't hear it in his shock.

His eyes were focused on Ernie.

Everything was happening in slow motion.

Ernie was leaning up against the wall, a blank expression on his face. His knees collapsed, and he slid down into a sitting position on the floor, then fell on his side.

What took just seconds seemed like minutes.

"Ernie! Ernie! Are you all right? Get up. Ernie? I'll never play with guns again. Ernie! Don't die! Please get up," pleaded Jerry, who then began to sob.

He was starting to realize that Ernie wouldn't be getting back up this time.

From that time on, Jerry's life would be shaped by this childhood accident. In their grief, his parents couldn't cope with Ernie's death and forbade anyone to speak about it. Jerry would live tortured by the accident, and he suffered bouts of depression and rage. He twice attempted suicide.

Parents forbade anyone to speak about it.

Growing up, Jerry never told anyone about his cousin, keeping the soul-damaging death a secret. His dad had forbade anyone in the family from talking about the death; and Jerry grew up carrying that burden, unable to tell anyone, not even his friends.

And his parents, in their grief, were unable to help Jerry cope.

FIRM BUT FAIR

Sam is a good boss and can easily motivate workers under him. Muscular and imposing at six feet three, he isn't a tyrant, earning his workers' respect and loyalty by being firm but fair. No problem between people is unsolvable, he now believes.

He has been at Fresno for just a month but has been able to pull the staff together despite his market now having twice the volume of produce and three times the workers than he had at his previous job in Sacramento.

He gives credit for his quick adjustment to another assistant manager, Tom Snyder, who is fifteen years his junior and possesses many of his new boss's traits. Tom was passed over for the job Sam took, but he holds no resentment. He has drawn comfort from the fact that Sam will retire in three years. Besides, he tells himself, this is an opportunity to learn from the more experienced Sam.

This morning, a Thursday, was mostly uneventful but was busy; and Sam's crew handled over five tons of produce by lunchtime.

Sam and Tom were located in the staff room at the market and were just starting their lunch when Tom asked about a story he had heard during the morning shift.

"Have you had a run-in with the wrecker next door?" Tom asked.

"Yes, a big one, I'm afraid," Sam replied. "It was the day before yesterday. You've got to watch out for him, you know. He can be as mean and as vicious as that dog of his."

"Well, what happened?" Tom asked.

As Sam starts to tell the story, he briefly pauses before recalling the vivid memory.

"I was the last to leave the market two nights ago," Sam related. "And had walked out to my car, which was parked across the fence from the crane. I was just opening the car door when I heard a creaking sound and looked up to see an arm pushing open the wrecking yard gate. I hadn't met the old man yet and waited a bit to say hello. But before I could say anything, a huge rottweiler leaped through the gate and came at me. The dog wore a spiked fighting collar and was barking and snarling as he rushed me. His lips were pulled back and his teeth were bared."

Sam continued, "The beast bit into the arm of my coat before I could jump into the car and close the door. He shook and twisted his head as if he was trying to get a better grip and sink his teeth in further. I yelled in the direction of the gate, 'Get him off of me.' I tried to swing the dog around, trying to shake it loose. Christ, he was powerful. He must have weighed seventy-five pounds."

Sam told Tom, "I heard hideous laughter from inside the wrecking yard and looked toward the gate. I could no longer see the old man but could hear him. 'Get him off! Get him off!' I screamed! The old man laughed again. It was crazy!

"'Get him, King. Get him,' the old man cried out," Sam recalled.

"Get him King. Get him." The market manager was amazed at the tenacity and aggressiveness of the rottweiler, but his initial surprise and fear had turned into anger.

"I lifted the dog on his hind legs and, with one movement, slammed him into the side of the car and freed myself. But in an instant, the dog was back up and charging again. I kicked him in the chest, knocking the wind out of him, all of which gave me the chance to leap into my car and close the door," Sam related.

Tom shuddered. "God, he could have killed you if he ever got you on the ground," Tom blurted out.

Sam continued, saying he was just starting the car when the dog smashed into the door's window, bounced off the car, then lunged again. "He jumped up on the hood and lunged at the windshield, biting and clawing, still trying to get at me. Jesus! He was as if he was trying to bite at my face through the glass," Sam said. "I'm glad that glass was there."

Sam's thoughts returned to the produce market staff room and to Tom, now sitting across the table from him with his mouth agape.

"Christ Almighty. You were lucky to get away from him!" Tom exclaimed. "Well, you drove away, right? I thought it was the old man you had the run-in with. What happened next?"

"I started my car and moved back a little, and the dog slipped off the hood," Sam said, picking up the story where he had left off. "I didn't see him for a second or two and looked down to see what gear I was in and shifted to go in reverse. I was backing away and looked up in my rear-view mirror, and suddenly there he was, about ten feet away. Son of a bitch. I thought I was rid of him, but he tried to jump onto the rear of my car. But by now I was going too fast. He hit the back of my car, then the rear window, before he bounced way over the top. Shit! I just wanted to get out of there. I looked ahead of me and saw him on the ground, not moving. I killed him!"

"No one should be able to keep a vicious dog like that around," Tom said. "Shit! It was good you killed him. Something bad could have happened to you. What about the old man?"

Sam paused a second as he recalled what followed. He could picture it clearly in his mind. "I stopped my car and went back toward the dog, reaching it at about the same time as the old man. His face was twisted in pain as he approached," Sam recalled sadly.

"King, oh, King," the old man wailed as he approached the dog's body. "You son of a bitch. Why did you kill him?"

"I didn't mean to kill him, but he attacked me," Sam blurted out in self-defense. "And he just jumped at me. Christ, he was mean. Why did you set him on me?"

The old man ignored what Sam was saying and reached down and picked the dog up in his arms. He was holding it like a baby, hugged it, and rocked it in his arms. He began to sob.

"Oh, King. You were my only friend," the old man cried as he turned and started back toward the wrecking yard, staggering with the heavy dog in his arms.

As the old man reached the gate, he turned and glared at Sam. "You dirty bastard," he said with venom. "Why did you kill him? I'll get you for this."

The rage disappeared from the old man's face, and he buried his face in the dog's coat and started to cry again, seemingly lost in his grief.

After a few seconds, the old man's mood changed again. Tears were still streaming down his cheeks and into his beard. He looked up at Sam, and his face was painted with hatred.

When he spoke, his voice no longer was broken by emotion. It was chilling and poisonous. "You bastard! Get your ass away from me," he demanded. "Go on. Get the fuck away from me."

"It wasn't my fault," Sam replied as the old man disappeared inside the wrecking yard.

Sam again focused on the staff room and on Tom. "And it wasn't my fault. What a crazy man."

Tom interjected, "Shit. What an experience."

"Really," Sam replied. "You know, even though I didn't deserve what he said, I feel sorry for that old man. But I'm sure he sicced that dog on me."

"That would fit the stories we hear about him," Tom said. "But the others weren't as extreme as this one."

Sam continued, "Well, I still feel sorry. I tried to go over there before work today to offer to get him a new dog. You know, we're neighbors, and I wouldn't want this to cause any problems in the future. But when I got here this morning, he was already up in his crane. I couldn't get his attention. Maybe I can get to talk to him today after work."

"I wouldn't go over there again," Tom advised. "He must be a bit crazy. About twenty years ago, another crane operator dropped a car that nearly finished off the old man. If he hadn't jumped out of the way, he would have been killed."

"What were his injuries?" Sam asked.

"He suffered a pretty serious blow to his head and ended up with a leg and shoulder smashed up," Tom replied. "He spent six months in the hospital and had to stay another two months at home to fully recuperate. At first, they didn't think he would make it."

Tom paused and recalled another story he'd heard.

"To make matters worse, while he was in the hospital, Sally, his wife, started seeing someone else. After he was released and returned home, she and the boyfriend kept screwing. That is, until the old man caught them. Well, he went berserk, they say. He was crazy with anger. He grabbed a poker, drove her lover from the house, and then nearly beat his wife to death with his fists. He blacked out, his attorney argued in court, and was found guilty of attempted murder and was in prison for seven years," Tom added.

"Well, I can see where catching his wife and lover would stir you up a bit," Sam reacted with sarcasm and a chuckle.

Tom interjected, "Other than his dog, the old man has been a recluse since then. He's still bitter and **"I've got to try to make peace."** won't let anyone come around. The only people you ever see him with are train workers who leave flatcars on the rail siding and truckers bringing in loads of wrecks."

"Well, I've got to try something to make peace," Sam interjected.

"Don't go over there tonight," Tom warned. "Let me try first. I've talked to him through the fence several times. It's just been cordial, but at least I'm a familiar face. Let me approach him for you," Tom implored. "But now that his dog is dead, I don't know what he'll do."

"Thanks for your help," Sam replied. "But don't take any chances. Hopefully, all he needs is someone to do him a little kindness."

Later that day, at nightfall, Sam again was the last person to leave for his car. When he got there, he heard an uproar from inside the old man's cabin. He heard a crash and an angry cry. Sam peered once more through the hole in the fence. There was another crash and the sound of splintering glass. A liquor bottle hit the ground outside the cabin.

"Sally, Sally. Why did you do it? I loved you," the old man wailed from inside the cabin. "But you got what you deserved, didn't you, you fuckin' whore. No slut is going to screw me around."

"Shit, he has really lost it," Sam reacted. "He's really sick."

"Oh, King. Oh, King. Why? You were my friend," the old man lamented.

Jerry then burst through the door of the shed; in his arms was the rigid body of the dog, its black coat tinged red by dried blood.

Sam just stared. The old man carried the body over to a hole behind the shed and put the animal down. He looked around.

Sam recoiled at the wildness he saw in those eyes and ducked down.

"Motherfuckers!" the old man screamed.

Sam heard running and looked up as the old man leaped up onto the tracks of the crane, jumped into the cab, and started the engine. He hoisted the bucket all the way to the top of the boom, swiveled the crane 180 degrees to the left, and let the bucket drop freely onto one of the cars. The claw grabbed and bit in. Window glass popped under the pressure. The top crumpled, and the hood sprung open.

Sam watched in awe.

"A beast. A terrible beast," he said softly to himself.

"A beast. A terrible beast." The beast lifted the car high and let it and the bucket crash down onto another wreck. The car was raised again, and the old man started swinging it back and forth by swiveling the crane cab on its base. At its highest swing, he released the cable, and the bucket-gripped car bombed into a stack of eight other cars, scattering them. The momentum of the swing momentarily lifted the crane's right track off the ground.

"This is madness," Sam observed, unable to remove his eyes from the scene. He realized that what he had witnessed that morning was being reenacted.

Jerry's face looked fleshless, and the eyes were blank. Again, it was a skull that peered out from under the mangled hard hat. The machine responded to the operator's manipulations with such quickness; the two moved as one.

If the machine were actually alive, the old man could be its brain, Sam thought to himself, frozen in awe.

Again, for an instant, he felt he might be looking into the past. Caught in the shadow of the crane's boom and the silver hue of the ending sunset, the glint of the old man's sweat, the rust of his beard, and caked blood gave him a metallic appearance. The old man appeared to be just another part of the steel machine.

Sam was so absorbed that at first, he hadn't realized that the crane had picked up another car and was again swinging it back and forth, seemingly shaking the car as a beast would its prey.

The crane again lifted on one track. Again it was on the verge of toppling.

Then something about the car caused Sam to lock his eyes on it. It had been cut and ripped and brutally mutilated in the old man's ritual but looked different than the other cars in the wrecking yard. Its body appeared newer than the other wrecks.

Sam stared, trying to determine what caught his eye.

"This is no wreck," Sam said loudly, stiffening against a ripple of fear and revulsion that swept over him. He became frozen by horror.

As the crane was lifting the car again, the car's front door popped open and fell off as the jaw gnawed deeper. From inside the front seat of the car appeared an arm, then another arm.

Sam realized there was someone lying in the front seat of the car.

A man started to slide off the seat in the swing of the bucket. He fell on the next swing and landed on the top of one of the stacks. He bounced like a rag doll onto the heap. He was a bloody mess but let out a gasp, a moan. Then he moved.

"Jesus, it's Tom," Sam screamed. "And that's his car. He must have come over here before me. The old man grabbed Tom and his car over the fence and tried to kill him. Jesus, he's crazy. I've got to get him out. He got him. I've got to get him out."

Sam looked back up at the old man. Gone was the emptiness in his eyes. The wildness had returned. Their eyes met.

"I'll go get help, Tom," Sam screamed while running over to his car. "I'll get help."

He jumped inside his car and tried to start it. But he had tried to insert the trunk key into the ignition in his haste and had to pull it out and re-insert the correct key. He started the engine and was about to shift into drive when something knocked the wind out of him. He gasped for air and momentarily couldn't breathe. He was being crushed. He blacked out for an instant, then came to and found himself pinned against the steering wheel. The roof was crushed and nearly touched the top of Sam's head.

Sam heard the screech of metal cutting through metal. The windows of his car popped, sending thousands of diamond-like fragments into his car.

"Oh Christ. He's got me now!" Sam cried out. "Got to get away." He jammed down on the accelerator and slipped the car into reverse. The tires squealed, then caught hold and propelled the car backward and away from the wrecking yard.

The old man had swung the bucket outside the wrecking yard and had grabbed Sam's car. Jerry was still trying to get a good grip on the car before lifting it when Sam's car started moving.

The first jerk of the car pulled out cable until the old man stopped the flow with the winch brake. The crane tottered a little in the struggle with the car, one track lifting up and then falling back, lifting up and then plunging back down.

The car was free for a few seconds; and Sam shifted into drive, turned the wheels, and gunned the engine again, building just enough momentum to cause a sudden jerk on the cable.

One track of the crane lifted. The car moved a bit and jerked again; the motor revved and the tires spun, but Sam could make no progress. The motor lugged and died. Sam could still feel the pressure from above, but all was quiet now.

He wriggled out of his trap against the steering wheel and squeezed into the passenger seat, crawling out of the car through the broken door window. He took a few steps away and looked back in awe at the wrecking yard.

He wriggled out of his trap.

The crane was on its side and smoke was pouring out of it. It had been toppled by the tug of the car. An explosion rocked the crane, which lifted and twisted momentarily as if in the final throes of death. Flames suddenly engulfed the machine.

"Where is Tom? Got to get him out," Sam said as he ran toward the wrecking-yard gate. He used his six-foot-three frame to hit it going full speed and smashed through.

Inside, he found Tom lying on the top of the car where he had fallen. He was still breathing, and it looked like his injuries were minor.

"You're going to be okay," Sam told Tom after surveying his injuries. "I'll get you help, but I've got to try and get the old man out."

"Go ahead. I'll be okay here," Tom said.

Sam forced himself to climb up on one track of the upended crane and stooped low to avoid the flames coming out of the partially opened cab door.

Looking inside, he saw the old man crushed in his seat by part of the boom, which had broken, then pierced the cab in the crash. The old man was hunched over and still gripping the boom controls. The eyes were empty.

"The skull," Sam said, sucking in a breath in reaction to the revolting sight.

Sam thought the old man was dead but still tried to get inside. He tried to open the cab door but was driven back by flames that leaped out at him. He jumped to the side and tried to reach the old man through a window, only to have to leap free the next instant when another explosion rocked the monster and knocked Sam off the track.

Sam picked himself up and ran from the fire, which had become an inferno, then stopped, turned, and stared at the crane, realizing there was nothing he could do now.

There was another blast. The monster quivered and shuddered, then the throes ended.

The beast was dead.

AUTHOR'S NOTES

The following resources were found to be valuable in my attempt to learn to deal with anger and lift myself out of depression.

McKay, Matthew, PhD and Peter Rogers, PhD. *Anger Hurts* and accompanying book *The Anger Control Workbook*. Oakland, CA: New Harbinger Publications, Inc. 2003 and 2000.

Chapters deal with "Getting Started: Emergency Anger Control"; "Understanding Your Anger"; "Trigger Thoughts"; and "Your Plan for Real-life Coping." My anger problems ranged from a lack of control that led to fist fights to near-road rage. Reviewer Jerry Defenbacher, PhD, points out that in these books, "the reader learns by showing and telling…rehearsing, trying out and modifying."

O'Connor, Richard, PhD. *Undoing Depression: What Therapy Doesn't Teach You and Medication Can't Give You*, 3rd ed. New York, Boston, and London: Little, Brown Spark. 2021.

William Styron, author of *Darkness Visible,* calls *Undoing,* "A balanced and persuasive work that explores the dark predicament of depression and the pathways toward help, with fresh insight."

Van der Kolk, Bessel, MD. *The Body Keeps the Score, Brain, Mind, and Body in the Healing of Trauma*. New York: Penguin Random House LLC, 2014.

For me, the most revealing was the revelation that the brain is impacted by overwhelming trauma (pages 2–3). Based on Dr. Van der Kolk's thirty years of experience, the book comprises five parts, including "The Rediscovery of Trauma," "The Minds of Children," and "Paths to Recovery."

President Franklin D. Roosevelt said, "Men are not prisoners of fate, but only prisoners of their own minds" in a speech on October 10, 1935.

ABOUT THE AUTHOR

This is the author's first work of fiction.

He is a retired journalist who worked for newspapers in Northern California for forty years, serving as a reporter, photographer, sports editor, and copy editor.

When he was eight years old, an overwhelming trauma and his family's reaction to it shaped his life. It wasn't until after his retirement that he learned the full effects of that trauma. In hindsight, they were life-changing. After discovering the depth of the problems the trauma caused, he started to work on major issues of anger, depression, and his solitary life.

In this novel, he focuses on two fictional characters to point out how trauma can affect veterans' lives.

He attempts to share this with readers to further the understanding of mental illness as well as help end the stigma placed on it by society.

He lives near his family in Northern California and enjoys fishing, photography, camping, and bowling.

Life in Crisis?

Call or text 988 if experiencing a mental health crisis.

Text 741-741 to reach a counselor for the National Alliance on Mental Illness (NAMI).

Call (800) 950-6264, the NAMI helpline.

For veterans and their loved ones:

Call (877) 927-8387.

Call 98844, then select option 1.

Symptoms of post-traumatic stress disorder

- Feeling upset by things that remind you of what happened
- Having nightmares, vivid memories, or flashbacks that make you feel like it's happening over again
- Feeling emotionally cut off from others
- Feeling numb or losing interest in things that you used to care about
- Feeling constantly on guard
- Feeling irritated or having angry outbursts
- Having trouble sleeping
- Having trouble concentrating
- Being jumpy or easily startled

Facts to consider

In the United States, one in five adults and one in six youth aged six to seventeen experience a mental health disorder each year.

On average, one person in the United States dies by suicide every eleven minutes.

(Sources: NAMI and US Department of Veteran Affairs)